Hello Benny!

by ROBIE H. HARRIS

illustrated by MICHAEL EMBERLEY

MARGARET K. McELDERRY BOOKS

NEW YORK   LONDON   TORONTO   SYDNEY   SINGAPORE

Margaret K. McElderry Books
An imprint of Simon & Schuster Children's Publishing Division
1230 Avenue of the Americas, New York, NY 10020

Book design by Michael Nelson
The text of this book is set in Lucida Casual.
The illustrations are rendered in watercolor, pastel, and pen and ink.

Printed in Hong Kong
2 4 6 8 10 9 7 5 3 1
LIBRARY OF CONGRESS CATALOGING-IN-PUBLICATION DATA
Harris, Robie H.
Growing up stories : Hello Benny! What it's like to be a baby / Robie H. Harris ;
illustrated by Michael Emberley.
p. cm.
Summary: Benny learns many things during the first year of his life.
Includes nonfiction information about infant development.
ISBN 0-689-83257-5
[1. Babies—Fiction. 2. Growth—Fiction.] I. Title: When Benny was a baby.
II. Emberley, Michael, ill. III. Title.
PZ7.H2436 Gr 2002
[E]—dc21
00-058741

For my mother
—M. E.

This one's for you—BEN!
—R. H. H.

Every child and grown-up was a baby. And babies and children become part of a family in different ways. Most babies are born into their family. Some babies and children are adopted into their family. There are many, many different kinds of families.

"Wha-wha-wha-whaaaaaaaaaah!" wailed Benny as he opened his eyes wide—and closed them. "Hello, Benny!" whispered his daddy. Benny had just been born! And he had just found out that light is bright.

When Benny opened his eyes again, his mommy was holding him tight. Benny looked at her face—for the very first time! He had never seen her face before! His mommy kissed his tiny fingers—and Benny opened his eyes even wider. His daddy kissed his nose—and Benny wiggled his tiny toes.

When a new baby cries, hearing the sound of a soft and quiet voice and being gently cuddled and touched feels good. This can make a new baby feel better—and even stop crying. When most new babies cry, they don't cry tears. They don't cry tears until they are a few weeks old.

CLOSE UP

KOOCHIE KOO!

Most new babies can see. Babies—even new babies—love to be held close and love to look at other people's faces most of all. Things that are farther away look blurry—not clear—to new babies until they are a few weeks older.

FAR AWAY

KOOCHIE KOO!

A few seconds later it was quiet. "Ooooooooooooooo . . . ooooooooooooooo" were the soft breathing sounds Benny made.

"Ooooooooooooooo, my sweetie pie," were the soft sounds his mommy whispered back.

Benny heard his mommy's voice and he turned his head towards her. He already knew the sound of her voice. When she touched his cheek and whispered, "I love you!" Benny opened his mouth wide and began to suck. Benny was only a few minutes old, but he already knew how to eat.

The only food new babies need is milk from their mother's breasts or from a bottle filled with special milk for babies. This special milk is made from cow's milk or soybeans. Breast milk and the special milk taste different from the milk we drink. The special milk has a stronger taste because extra vitamins, salt, sugar, and fat have been added to it.

MMMM!! TOO BAD LITTLE BABIES CAN'T DRINK CHOCOLATE MILK SHAKES!

YUCK!! THAT'S NO MILK SHAKE!

IT'S TRUE, SHE DOESN'T LIKE LEMONS!

THAT'S WHY SHE'S MAKING A SOUR FACE!

New babies like the taste and smell of some things better than others. They will turn their heads towards the smell of their mother's breast milk. But they do not like the taste and smell of sour things. If they smell something sour, like a lemon, they squiggle up their noses, close their mouths, and turn away.

When Benny was one week old, his cousin Lizzie came to meet him. Lizzie stared at Benny. Then she slowly stuck her tongue out at Benny—and held it out—two times in a row. Then Benny stuck his tongue out too—and Lizzie laughed. Benny was just a tiny baby, but he could copy his big cousin!

Then Lizzie grabbed a bright yellow duck, held it in front of Benny, and sang, "Quack! Quack!" Benny waved his arms, kicked his feet, squinched up his face—and pooped. Lizzie laughed again. While Benny's daddy changed his diaper, Lizzie moved the duck from side to side and up and down—and Benny's eyes and head followed the duck.

Lots of kids and grown-ups think all that new babies do is eat, sleep, pee, poop, and get their diapers changed. They do spend a lot of time doing those things. But most new babies can also hear, see, smell, suck, taste, yawn, sneeze, burp, hiccup, touch, grasp, kick, move, cry, gurgle, and blink.

WOW!

THIS ENOUGH DIAPERS FOR THIS AFTERNOON?

SHE'S NOT THTICKING OUT HER TONGUE THITH THIME!

WELL, THAT IS THE SIXTY-FOURTH TIME YOU'VE DONE IT!

If a new baby sees you open your mouth, yawn, or stick out your tongue and hold it out, sometimes the baby will copy you and do the same thing. No one knows exactly how or why a new baby can do that. Most new babies can also follow something that moves slowly—with their eyes and their head.

Benny made lots of noises—snorts, sneezes, snores, grunts, gurgles, cries, hiccups, and burps—from the moment he was born. Benny made lots of faces, too—even smiles. All those sweet faces and noises made people smile at Benny a lot—because they loved him a lot. But Benny was still too little to smile back.

One day, many weeks after he was born, Benny's mommy sang, "Ohhhh, be-bop-a-Benny! I love my Ben-ny baby!" Benny gurgled—and his mommy smiled a big smile. Benny opened his eyes wide, curled up the corners of his mouth—and smiled back. This was the very first time Benny smiled back at another person!

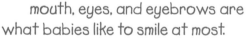

New babies or babies who are only a few weeks old make all kinds of faces—happy, lopsided, smiley, adorable, pouty, sad, and mad faces. But if you smile at a new baby or at a baby who is only a few weeks old, usually the baby is not able to smile back at you yet, even though they love to look at smiling faces.

If you smile, talk, whisper, or sing to a baby who is many weeks old, most often the baby will smile back at you. For a few months after that, babies smile at everyone they meet and sometimes even at a photo. People who smile, make noises, and move their mouth, eyes, and eyebrows are what babies like to smile at most.

One morning, Benny's mommy put him on his tummy—and sat right next to him. Benny lifted his chin up, looked around, gurgled "Eeh"—and put his head right back down. Benny looked like a turtle when he did that. That day, whenever he wasn't sleeping, or eating, or having his diaper changed—Benny was doing chin-ups!

One night, Benny's daddy lay down on the floor, lifted his chin up, and gurgled "Eeh"—just like Benny. Now his daddy looked like a turtle. Benny got so excited that he began to drool and hiccup—and lift his chin up too. Then Benny put his head down to take a rest. Chin-ups were hard work!

...42 ... 43 ... 44 ...

Once babies do something new, they often do it over and over again because they are practicing what they have learned—and because it's fun to do something new.

LET'S SEE ... HICCUPING ... HERE IT IS! IT MEANS A BABY IS EXCITED OR TIRED. BUT SO DOES KICKING, WAVING, DROOLING, OR ...

THE BABY BOOK

HIC!

Drooling, hiccuping, breathing fast, or kicking their legs and waving their arms are ways young babies show us how excited they are when they do something new. But it can also be their way of saying, "I'm tired and I want to stop doing this."

Whenever Benny got tired, or mad, or hungry, or cranky, he'd stuff his fingers or thumb in his mouth—and make himself feel better. When he was feeling happy, sometimes he'd stuff his fingers or thumb in his mouth too—because it felt good.

A hug or a kiss or a cuddle can make a baby feel good or feel better. Often, babies can make themselves feel better by sucking on their thumbs, or fingers, or fists—or even on a toy.

Babies put everything they can into their mouths—even their fingers and toes and other people's fingers or noses. This helps them learn whether something feels rough or smooth, soft or hard, comfy or not— or tastes good or yucky, or hot or cold.

THAT'S HOW HE LEARNS ABOUT NOSES!

HE GWABBED BY DOSE!

When Benny was a little older, he could put his foot in his mouth. First he'd reach for his foot and grab it with both hands. Then he'd put his big toe in his mouth. Then he'd try to put almost all his toes in his mouth. Benny looked like a pretzel when he did that! For a while, Benny's thumbs and fingers and toes and feet were his favorite toys.

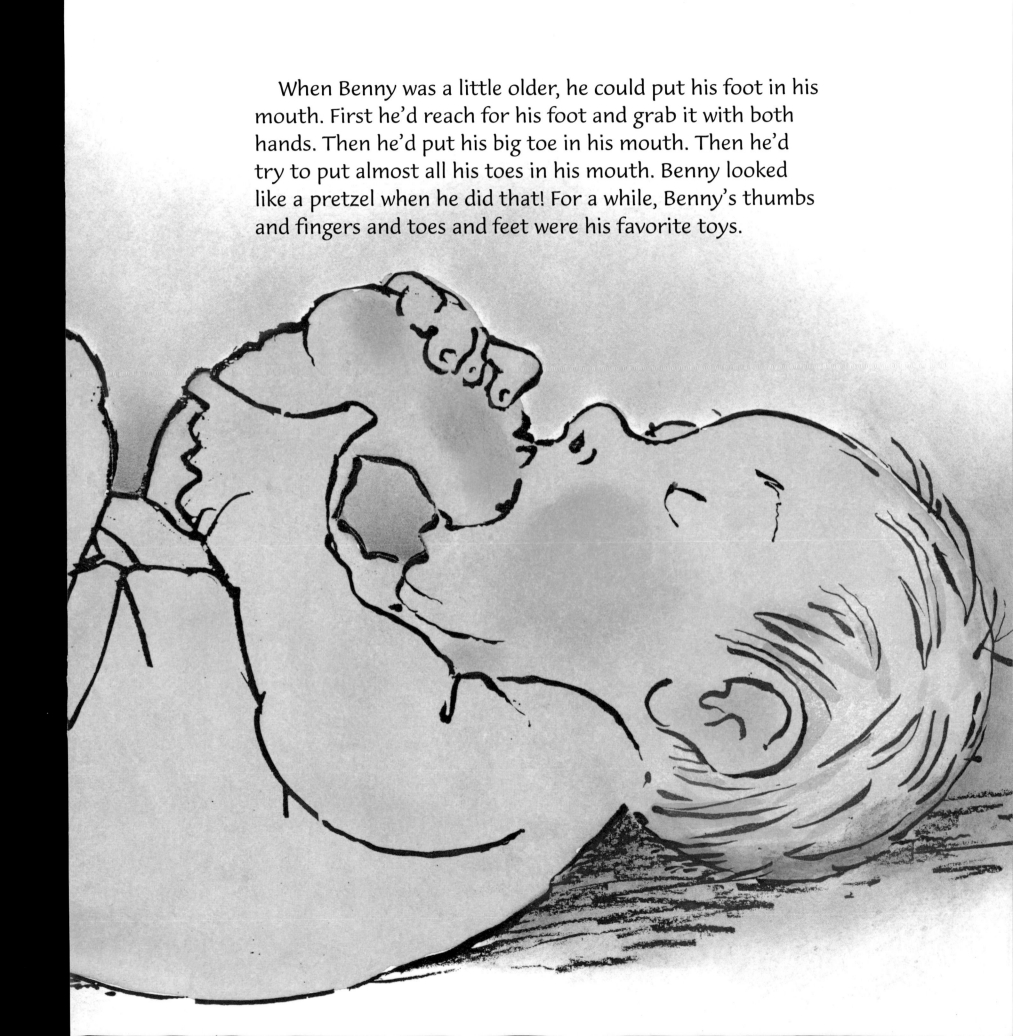

The first time Benny rolled over from his tummy to his back, no matter how hard or how many times he tried, he couldn't roll back over. He got so mad, he kicked his feet and cried. One night, Benny finally did roll back over. He got so excited, he laughed the biggest belly laugh. His laugh made his mommy and daddy laugh.

A-A-A-A-AH!!

WHAT'S WRONG? WHY IS HE CRYING?

UMMM, LET'S SEE ... THE BABY IS HUNGRY. UH, WAIT! ... OR HURT ... OR ... HOT ... OR COLD ... OR NEEDS A NEW DIAPER ...

AH-A-A-A-A

THE BABY BOOK

Crying is a baby's way of telling us if he or she feels hungry, angry, tired, bored, lonely, scared, hurt, or sick—or too hot or cold, or needs a diaper changed—or just wants to play with someone—or have some fun—or be picked up and cuddled.

Babies love to laugh—tiny laughs as well as belly laughs. Seeing and hearing other people talk, laugh, or smile can make a baby laugh. Being surprised—like when you play peek-a-boo—can make a baby laugh.

PEEK-A-BOO!

HEE! HEE! HEE!

I'M NEXT!

For a few weeks, whenever Benny was on his tummy, he looked like an airplane ready to take off. He would sputter "Ph-ph-phhhhhh!" and wave his arms and feet in the air. But his tummy would stay on the ground. He was moving a lot and staying in one place. He was working hard and having fun. But Benny wasn't going anywhere—yet!

Sometimes, Benny sounded like an opera singer. When his daddy sang "Laaaaaaaaaa," Benny answered "Aaaaaaaaaaah." When Benny cooed "Gooooooooooh," his daddy whispered "Booooooooo!"

Babies love to make noise because it's fun. When they do make a noise, most times someone will come and pick them up, or play with them, or talk to them. The more you talk to a baby, the more sounds a baby makes back. Talking with a baby helps a baby learn to talk.

Babies also learn that when they do something, something else can happen. When they shake a rattle or shriek, they make a noise. When they cry or shriek, people come and help them. When they make sounds or smile, people make sounds and smile back at them.

INTERNATIONAL BABY BABBLE CONVENTION

Young babies all around the world make a lot of the same sounds, no matter what language is spoken to them.

One night—in the middle of the night—Benny woke up
and began to make more new noises. "Ya-ya-ya-ya-yaaaaaa,"
he sang to the dinosaurs hanging over his crib. "Ba-ba-ba-
ba-ba-ba-ba!" he babbled to his book. "Muh-muh-muh-muh-
muh-muh-muh!" he muttered to his rattle—and then he
shook it! But soon it was quiet again. Benny had fallen
asleep again.

The first time Benny sat up all by himself, he really wasn't sitting up. He was sitting over—and humming "Mmmmm." But then Benny fell over on his side and cried. So his mommy sat him up again. Benny stopped crying and hummed "Mmmmm" again—until he fell over and cried again.

When babies learn to move in a new way—roll over, sit up, crawl, or stand up—they get excited and feel good. Now they can go places they've never been—behind the couch, or under a chair or table, or through a door—and see things they've never seen. Sooner or later they learn to go up and down stairs.

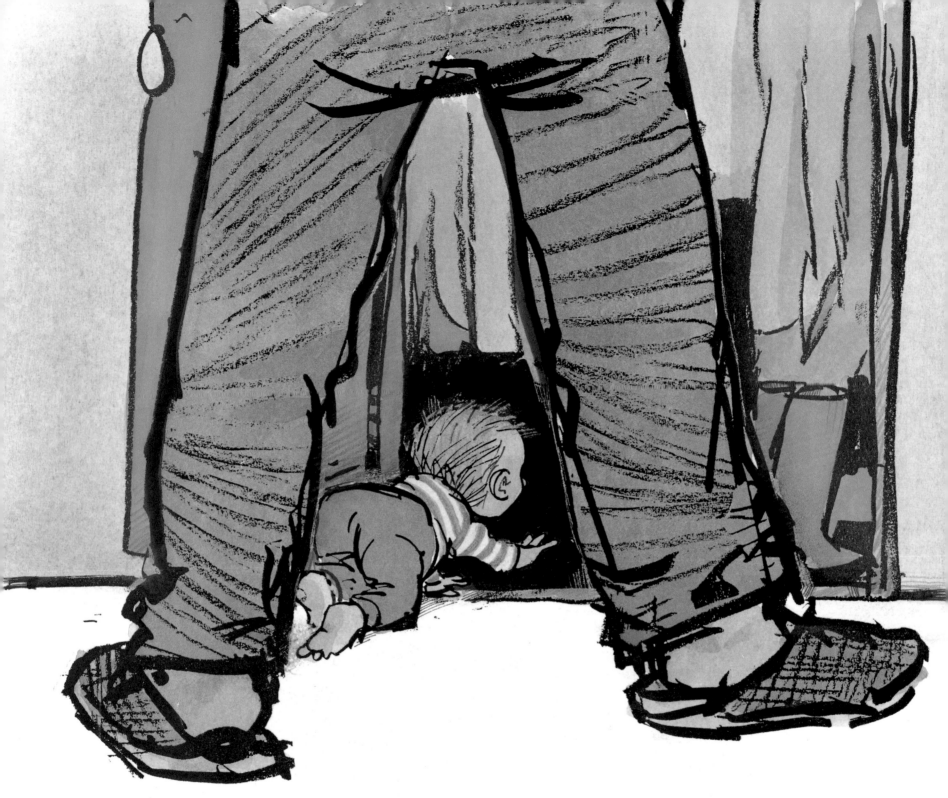

One day, Benny got up on his hands and knees and rocked back and forth. Suddenly he began to crawl for the very first time—until he got stuck under a chair. "Eeeeeekkkkk!" he shrieked. His daddy picked up the chair. Benny crawled through his daddy's legs and into the hall closet. Now Benny could go almost everywhere—all on his own!

Early one morning, Benny spent a long time looking at a baby's face. Then he smiled at the baby's face. The baby smiled back—and Benny yelled, "Ooh!" Benny smiled at the baby again—and the baby smiled back again. The smiley face in the mirror was Benny's face. But Benny didn't know that!

That night, when Benny's grandma hid her face under a napkin, Benny giggled. Then she made a funny face. Benny giggled again, grabbed her nose—and gave her a wet, drooly kiss. But if anyone looked at Benny with a sad, or mad, or angry, or grumpy face, he'd feel sad, or mad, or angry, or grumpy—until someone gave him a hug and a kiss.

IT'S OK... HE JUST DOESN'T KNOW YOU YET.

AAH! AAH! AAAAAH!

When babies are little, they smile at almost everybody. When they are older, if a person they have never seen before, or don't remember seeing before, looks at them or talks to them, they may cry or look away, and not smile back.

Many babies love to make sounds when people talk to them. Making sounds is a baby's way of "talking" to another person—or even to a toy. Many babies make sounds or try out new sounds, even when no one is in the same room with them. Making sounds is also their way of playing and having fun.

BUH-BUH-BUH! NA-NA-NA!

WHO IS SHE TALKING TO?

NO ONE. SHE'S JUST PRACTICING.

BUH-BUH BUH! NA-NA-NA!

Benny knew what he liked and didn't like to eat. Whenever he ate a banana, he'd squish it with his hands, stuff it in his mouth, mush it up, and smack his lips. Then he'd grin—and everyone could see Benny's first two brand-new teeth. Benny loved bananas!

Babies find out about things by using their whole hand to grab, pick up, drop, throw, squish, turn, tickle, touch, and squeeze things. They also smell things, put things in their mouths, and taste them. Once babies can use their thumb and finger to pinch things, they can pick up smaller things and look at, play with, and find out about more new things.

But he hated peas! If anyone tried to feed him cooked peas, Benny would slowly push the peas out of his mouth with his tongue. Or he'd spit them out fast. Or he'd shut his mouth tight. Or he'd shake his head back and forth. Benny did like to pick up cooked peas with his thumb and finger and squish them. He loved the way that felt!

Making an angry face, banging fists, waving arms, kicking feet, or shrieking are ways babies tell us they feel angry. Giving a kiss or smile, cuddling up, or making sounds like "e-e-e-e-e" or "oh-oh-oh" or babbling sounds like "buh-buh" or "guh-guh" are ways babies tell us they feel good.

IS HE MAD?

WHAT DID YOU SAY?

EEEEEEEEEEEEEEEEKKK!!!

EEEEEE

One morning, Benny pointed to a cow in his favorite book and said, "Dada!" His daddy laughed, pointed to himself, and said, "I'm Dada!"

Benny said "Dada!" again, pointed to his daddy, and laughed too. This time, Benny was "talking" about his daddy. This time, "Dada" was Benny's very first real word! His daddy was so excited, he gave Benny two big kisses.

All around the world, most babies about a year old say words that sound like "Dada" and "Mama," no matter what language their families speak. At first, babies say these sounds because they are trying out all the sounds they can make and it's fun. Later they learn that "Mama" means "Mommy" or "Dada" means "Daddy."

A few weeks later, Benny's mommy was reading a new book to him and the telephone rang. His mommy stopped reading and went to answer it. Benny cried. Then he waved "bye-bye" to his mommy—and to his book. But his mommy came right back. When Benny saw her, he stopped crying. And she read the whole book to him again.

When older babies wave "bye-bye," they often think that who or what they just saw may have disappeared—and may not come back. That's why they may feel sad or angry for a bit when someone they love stops playing with them, or goes into another room, or leaves. Often babies try to call after or follow that person to get them to come back.

One afternoon, Benny grabbed the legs of his mommy's chair and pulled himself up until he was standing up—for the very first time! His legs were wobbling and shaking. And he was smiling and laughing. But suddenly Benny didn't look like a little baby anymore.

A few weeks later, Benny let go of his daddy's hands and took two steps on his own—for the very first time! Benny felt so good that he smiled and clapped his hands—and fell down on his bottom. Benny wasn't smiling anymore. But he was getting ready to walk—all on his own.

When babies first stand, most can't sit back down without falling. Soon, they learn to stick out their bottoms first, so when they sit back down, they won't fall down. Once they can stand, babies take small steps—holding on to a table, a sofa, or a person. Next, they step from one thing to another—long before they can walk on their own.

Most babies crawl before they walk. Some never crawl at all, but pull themselves up until they are standing—and then walk. Most walk on their own for the first time sometime after their first birthday. Some walk on their own before their first birthday.

On Benny's first birthday, when everyone sang "Happy Birthday!"—he sang, "Bir-eeeee! Bir-eeeee!" Then he grabbed a handful of cake and shoved it in his mouth. Soon he had cake all over his face and in his hair. Benny loved licking the cake off his fingers and lips—and eating the ice cream with one hand—and banging his spoon with the other.

While cousin Lizzie opened his presents, Benny tore up the wrapping paper and threw it in the air. Then his grandma blew Benny a kiss. And he blew her a kiss—and yawned. Soon he fell asleep on his grandma's lap. On his first birthday, Benny was 1. Benny was GROWING UP!

By the time they are about one year old—or soon after—many babies can say two or three words. Some don't say any words yet. One-year-olds can understand more words than they can say. They probably know what words like "no," "dog," "shoe," "baby," "bye-bye," and "cookie" mean—even though they may not be able to say those words or lots of other words yet.

Babies and children often cuddle up with a "lovey"—a special, soft, cuddly blanket, quilt, scarf, cloth, or stuffed animal—to help them go to sleep, or feel safe, or feel comfy, or feel that everything will be okay. They also love to be cuddled by someone who loves them.

THANK YOU
FOR SHARING YOUR EXPERTISE AND AFFECTION FOR BABIES WITH US!

Naomi S. Baron, Ph.D., professor of linguistics, American University, Washington, D.C.

Marjorie Beegley, Ph.D., senior research associate, Child Development Unit, Children's Hospital; assistant professor of pediatrics, Harvard Medical School, Boston, MA

Sarah Birss, M.D., child analyst and pediatrician, Cambridge, MA

Kate Buttenwieser, M.S.W., social worker, Children's Hospital, Boston, MA

Deborah Chamberlain, M.S., research associate, Norwood, MA

Eileen Costello, M.D., assistant clinical director of pediatrics, Boston University School of Medicine; pediatrician, Dorchester House, Dorchester, MA

Sally Crissman, science educator, Shady Hill School, Cambridge, MA

Gerald Hass, M.D., pediatrician, Cambridge, MA; physician-in-chief, South End Community Center, Boston, MA

Ben Harris, M.Ed., elementary school teacher, New York, NY

Bill Harris, parent, Cambridge, MA

David Harris, M.S.Ed., prekindergarten/kindergarten teacher, New York, NY

Emily Berkman Harris, M.D., pediatrician, New York, NY

Hilary Grand Harris, parent, New York, NY

Robyn Heilbrun, parent, Salt Lake City, UT

Margot Kaplan-Sanoff, Ed.D., associate clinical professor of pediatrics; codirector, Healthy Steps, Boston University Medical Center, Boston, MA

Ellen Kelly, director, The Cambridge-Ellis School, Cambridge, MA

Elizabeth A. Levy, children's book author, New York, NY

Alicia Lieberman, Ph.D., professor of medical psychology, University of California at San Francisco, San Francisco, CA

Linda C. Mayes, M.D., associate professor of child psychiatry/pediatrics and psychology, Yale University Child Study Center, New Haven, CT

Steven J. Parker, M.D., pediatrician, associate professor of pediatrics, Boston University School of Medicine; director of behavior and developmental pediatrics, Boston Medical Center, Boston, MA

Janet Patterson, kindergarten teacher, Shady Hill School, Cambridge, MA

Jeree Pawl, Ph.D., director, Infant Parent Program, University of California at San Francisco, San Francisco, CA

James Pustejovsky, Ph.D., associate professor of computer science, Department of Computer Science, Brandeis University, Waltham, MA

Carol Sepkoski, Ph.D., developmental psychologist, Cambridge, MA

Karen Shorr, M.A.T., prekindergarten teacher, The Brookwood School, Manchester, MA

Edward Z. Tronick, Ph.D., chief, Child Development Unit, Children's Hospital, Boston, MA; associate professor of pediatrics, Harvard Medical School, Boston, MA

Barry Zuckerman, M.D., chairman, Department of Pediatrics, Boston University School of Medicine, Boston City Hospital, Boston, MA

Pamela Meyer Zuckerman, M.D., pediatrician, Brookline, MA